Written by
Susan Abrahams

Illustrated by
Roberta M. Rivera

Publishers Cataloging-in-Publication Data

Abrahams, Susan.
Hal, the Hamptons hound / written by Susan Abrahams ; illustrated by Roberta M. Rivera.
p. cm.
Summary: Hal, a detective bloodhound, works a case to find a poodle puppy named Pucci.
ISBN-13: 978-1-60131-068-2
[1. Bloodhound—Fiction. 2. Dogs—Juvenile fiction. 3. Detective and mystery stories.] I. Rivera, Roberta M., ill. II. Title.
2010922505

Copyright © 2010 Susan Abrahams
Printed and bound in the United States of America
First printing 2010

115 Bluebill Drive
Savannah, GA 31419
United States
(888) 300-1961

To order additional copies, please go to www.halthehamptonshound.com

All rights reserved. No part of this book may be reproduced or transmitted in any form or by any means, electronic or mechanical, including photocopying, recording or by an information storage and retrieval system—except by a reviewer who may quote brief passages in a review to be printed in a magazine, newspaper or on the web—without permission in writing from the publisher.

This book was published with the assistance of the helpful folks at DragonPencil.com.

To my loving and supportive husband, Joel,
who kept "hounding" me to write
Hal, The Hamptons Hound
And the Case of the Missing Puppies.

Susan Abrahams

In loving memory to my father, Bob Gallagher,
who read, sang and taught me the magic of
storytelling when I was a child.

Roberta Rivera

My name is Hal. I'm a cop. A bloodhound. A blue-blood hound with the nose to prove it. My beat is the Hamptons.

When a case has few facts and a lot of hunches, my honker comes in handy. I can sniff out trouble from miles away.

I eat prime leftovers from fine restaurants like Babette's and Nick and Toni's.

I slurp water at Starbarks. Sometimes I take a snooze with the cats in the window of BookHampton. It's a quiet life. That is until the summer comes and the city folk drive out East. The traffic is terrible. But for me, the main problem is lost pets.

Those city slicker cats and dogs have never been outside without a leash. Someone opens the door and they scram. They're lost. That's where I come in. My job is to find them.

Last summer I had my most puzzling case:

1:30 a.m.

It was Sunday, July 2nd.

It was hot in the Hamptons. I was working the night shift, helping a turtle cross the street, when I got a call on my walkie-talkie.

It was from my partner, Tuesday. She's a cat. A tabby with attitude. I call her Tuesday because I rescued her on a Tuesday. Makes sense. Back to the call.

"Hal," said Tuesday, "we just got a call from a poodle in distress. Her name is Princess. Her puppy, Pucci, has been dognapped."

"Sure she isn't lost?" I asked.

"Pretty sure. I read in the *East Hampton Star* that the pup is starring in a Broadway show called *Guys and Dogs*."

"So?" I said. "We have lots of famous pooches here in the summer."

"Yeah," said Tuesday, "but this one's different. Seems Pucci's a dancer too. Her paws are insured for two million biscuits."

"Hmm," I said. "Sounds suspicious. Did you answer the call?"

"Yes. I sent out an APB, All Poodles Bulletin, with her description."

"Good work. Any witnesses?"

"No."

"Okay. Let's go visit the mother. Maybe she can tell us something."

2:30 a.m.

We arrived at the residence. It was at the ocean. We found the poodle lounging on a chaise. She was dazzling. The moon reflected on her diamond-crusted collar. I was momentarily blinded.

"Hello, Ma'am," I said. "I'm Sergeant Hal. Are you Pucci's mother?"

"Yes," she said, blowing into a monogrammed hankie.

"Did you see anything?"

"No. I was having a manicure and pedicure at the time. I use Fire Hydrant Red."

"Just the facts, Ma'am. When did you see your pup last?"

"About two hours ago, when I tucked Pucci into bed." She blew hard into the handkerchief again. HHHONK!!!!!!!!!!!!!!

"Can we see Pucci's room?"

The dame led us there.

Pucci had a fancy canopied bed with perfumed sheets. Shar-Pei #5. I'd know that scent anywhere.

"Have you noticed anything suspicious lately, Ma'am?"

"I don't think so."

"We'll need you downtown, so we can show you some mutt shots. Maybe you can pick out the dognapper. In the meantime, we're going to dust for pawprints."

3:30 a.m.
We took Princess downtown to look through the books. She was dazzling, but her memory was fuzzy. Figures. Princess gave us a clue. Seems the pup liked yachts. We decided to cover the docks on Three Mile Harbor.

Sometimes I caught a whiff of Shar-Pei #5, but the scent led nowhere.

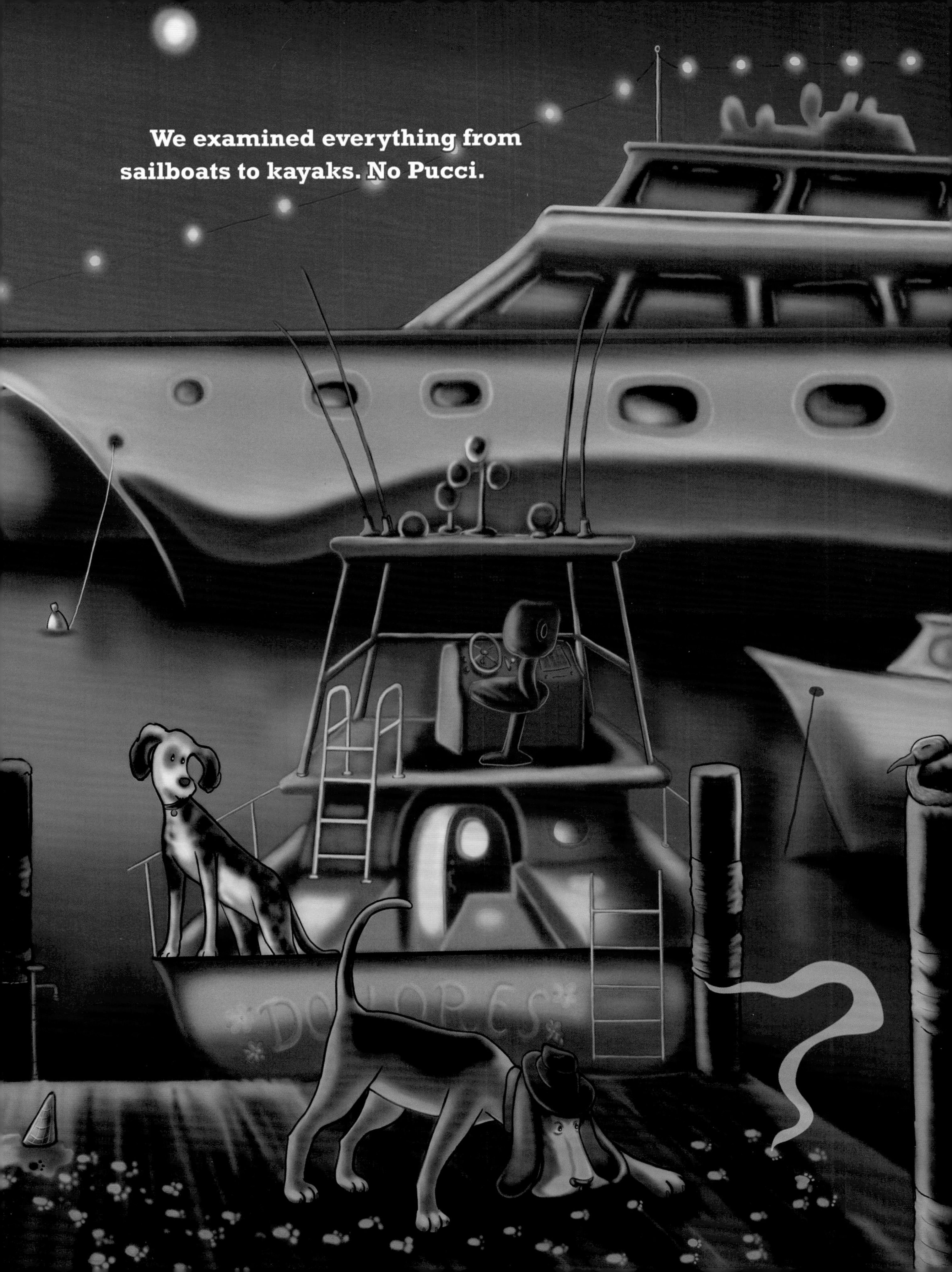

We examined everything from sailboats to kayaks. No Pucci.

4:32 a.m.

We got another phone call. Another missing puppy. This time it was a show dog named Roscoe the III. A cockapoodle.

I thought they were talking about a rooster. It was one of those fancy designer dogs. Half poodle, half cocker spaniel. I started to worry. It seemed the dognapper had struck again.

4:54 a.m.

We got a break. A boxer called. Said he knew something about the missing pups. We met him at his gym on Hog Creek Road.

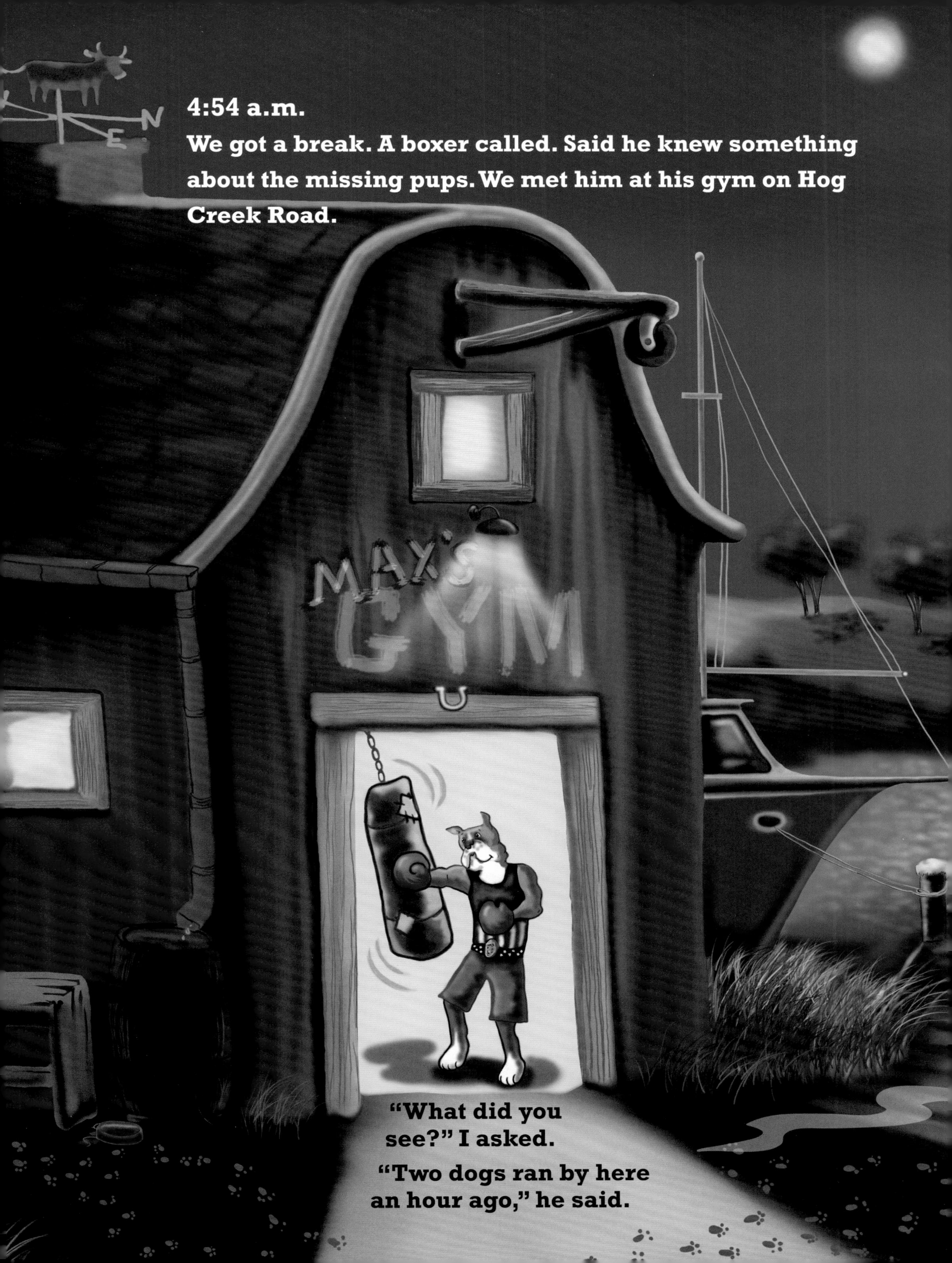

"What did you see?" I asked.

"Two dogs ran by here an hour ago," he said.

"Were they being chased?"

"Didn't see anyone, but they were headed toward the marinas. Let me go with you. I could be a big help. I used to be a heavyweight contender. My name is Max 'The Bear' Boxer. Remember me?"

"Can't say that I do, Sir. Sorry, can't let you come along," I said. "Company rules. You might bark up the wrong tree. But thanks for the tip."

5:16 a.m.

We headed back toward Three Mile Harbor. There was one marina left to cover, the Maidstone.

We planned a stakeout. We called for backup.

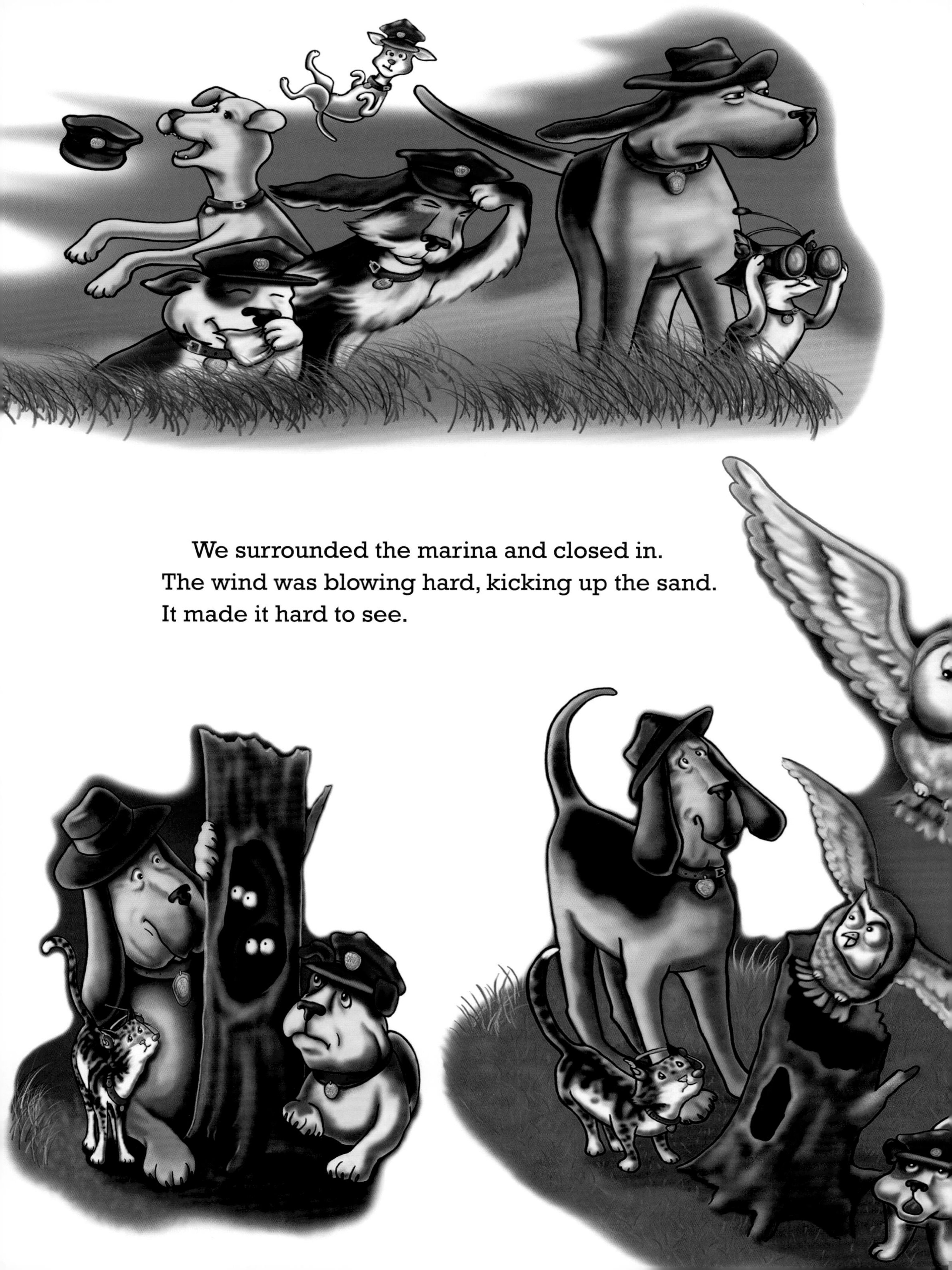

We surrounded the marina and closed in.
The wind was blowing hard, kicking up the sand.
It made it hard to see.

There were a few sightings, but they were just nibbles.

No pups. I was doggone tired. All I could think of was poor Princess. Suddenly, my nose smelled Shar-Pei #5.

5:59 a.m.
We followed the scent. It led us down the beach.

We were close.
I could tell.

My nose twitched now. It itched. I scratched.
I signaled the pack to hide in the dunes.

Slowly I pulled back the beach grass. What did I see? Two dogs rubbing noses. It was Pucci and Roscoe! They hadn't been dognapped after all. It was just a case of puppy love.

I was glad it all turned out okay. Tuesday took the puppies home to the waiting paws of their parents. I needed some chow.

My walkie-talkie buzzed again. It was Tuesday. "Sorry, Boss," she said. "Just got a call from headquarters; there's a dog making a ruckus at the Palm."

"I'll meet you there."

6:30 a.m. I raced down Main Street to the Palm Restaurant.

It was dark and quiet. My nose sensed trouble.

"SURPRISE!"

I whizzed around, my paws ready for action. The lights came on. Princess, Pucci, Roscoe, Tuesday, and my deputies were all there.

They threw me a surprise party! Princess had ordered all of my favorite leftovers and set up a table in the backyard by the hydrangeas.

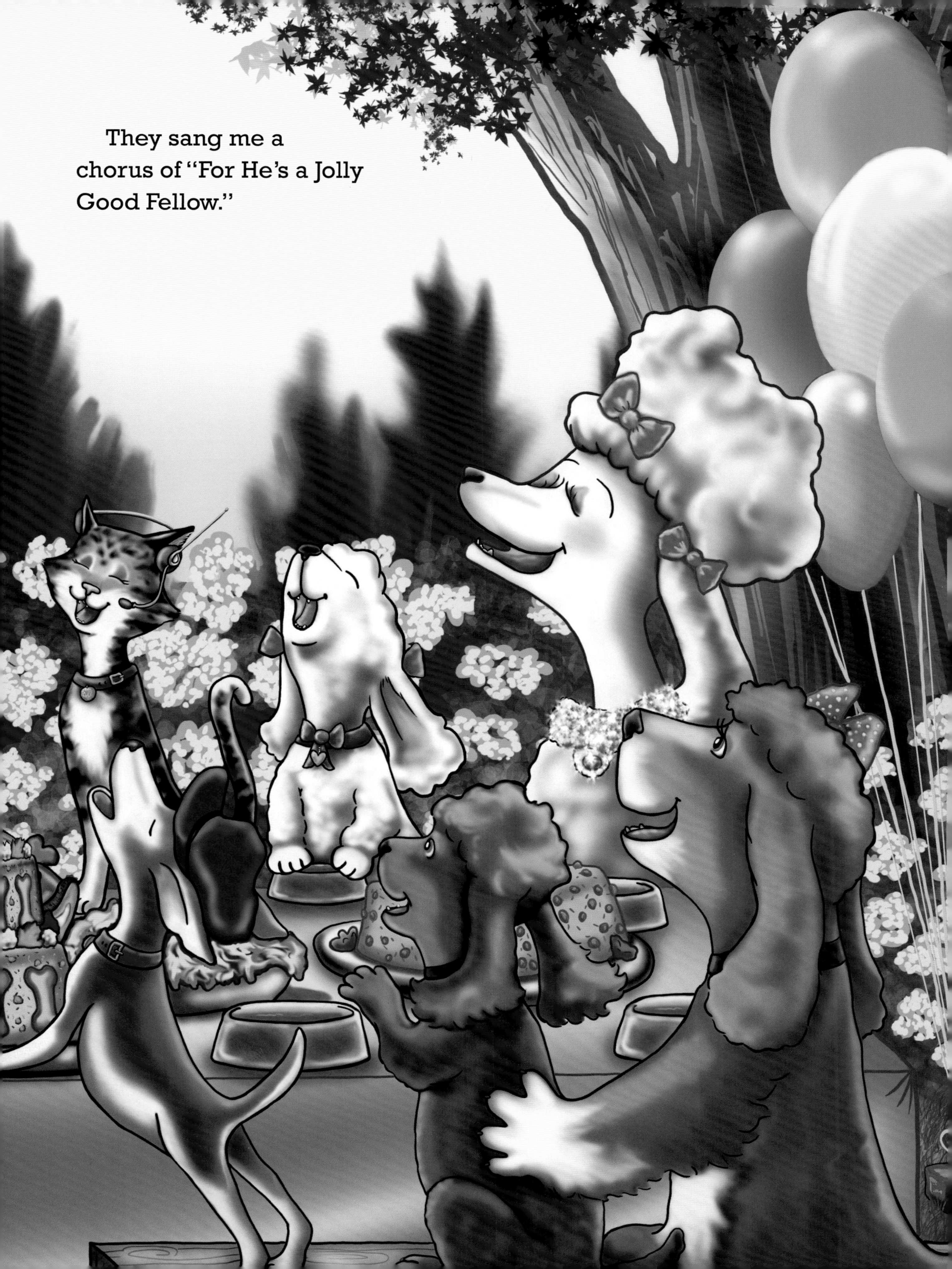

They sang me a chorus of "For He's a Jolly Good Fellow."

We chowed down on T-bones and creamed spinach. Princess snuggled next to me.

But that's another story.